Ivy-Lou
and the
Spooky Shoe

Written and illustrated by
Alana Josephson

This book is dedicated
to my family members,
especially the furry ones.

Ivy-Lou has been waiting for this all year.

But never did she think she'd be in such fear.

Surely Halloween couldn't be this spooky.

Every other year has just been plain old kooky.

The story of Ivy-Lou begins
on a cold Halloween night,

with no one around,
not even a kitty in sight.

The only one with me
is my Ivy-Lou

and that's all I need
and know to be true.

Ivy-Lou and I
spend hours collecting candy,

not knowing one day
it would actually come in handy.

12

The further we go,
the eerier the feeling.

Then Ivy-Lou whispers, "are you
hearing what I'm hearing"?

Spooked by the sound,
I take a step back.

Could this be a bear
waking up from its nap?

16

Yet all we can hear
is tap, tap, tap...

I start to feel
worried and confused

until Ivy-Lou says,
"I think it was just a shoe"!

20

We call out to see
if anyone is there,

never did we think
we'd get such a scare!

23

In the corner of her eye,
Ivy-Lou spots a shoe,

and thinks that taking it
is a good thing to do!

But in a few minutes
the shoe starts to glow,

did we make a mistake
taking something we don't know?

We hurry home,
dropping candy as we run,

surely I thought
this night would be more fun!

Ghouls, goblins, or zombies
could be hiding at every turn,

yet Ivy-Lou just doesn't seem
to be very concerned!

Finally, we make it home
and run inside,

thinking this will be
a safe place for us to hide!

We were wrong because
within just a few,

we got to see the magic
of Ivy-Lou and the spooky shoe...

Staring at the shoe
makes Ivy-Lou hungry,

next thing you know,
part of it's in her tummy!

The spooky shoe
changes our lives,

after only one bite
we're up in the sky!

Flying around
we feel invincible,

hopefully, we don't get caught
by the school principal!

Ivy-Lou and I wonder,
is this a spell?

Who would have thought
we could fly so well!

Flying in the sky
goes on for hours,

but soon we'll get to see
the real spooky powers!

From graves to caves
and everything in between,

the spooky shoe takes us on a
journey with much to be seen.

Soaring as high
as bats and birds.

Our friends will think
this is absurd!

But after a few hours,
the magic begins to wear off,

I guess now
we'll just have to walk!

Hidden away
we see a clue,

could it be something
for my Ivy-Lou?

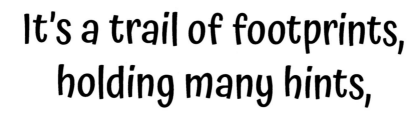

It's a trail of footprints,
holding many hints,

and Ivy-Lou thinks
that we should follow it!

55

The trail leads us to the owner
of the shoe and a good friend of mine,

his name just happens to be
Frankenstein!

Frankenstein wants
his spooky shoe back,

but we counteroffer
with our Halloween snacks...

To our surprise,
Frankenstein agrees,

and trades his spooky shoe
for our magical treats!

The adventures of Ivy-Lou
end with a magical twist,

can't every Halloween
be like this?

63

Something as simple as a shoe
changed her life.

The magic within it
let her take flight.

Ivy-Lou saw things
she never thought she would.

This Halloween ended
just like it should!

About Alana

Alana is a writer who specializes in short stories for children based on real-life events and characters.

She loves to share her experiences in a way that connects to readers.

Josephson had pets her whole life and is keen on documenting her youngest puppy's early years.

Her next goal is to study in Paris and pursue her modeling career.

About Ivy-Lou

Ivy-Lou is a 1-year-old Havanese from Florida who loves her sisters and cousin Henry!

Her main hobby is collecting shoes to play with and eventually destroy.

She also enjoys making new friends at the groomer and dog park!

Ivy-Lou is looking forward to being her mom's sidekick for all her future adventures.

Acknowledgements

Special thanks to my mother for always encouraging me to follow my passions.

Special thanks to Marisa for helping me with my projects.

Special thanks to Milena Ivanov for assisting me with the graphics.

Extra special thanks to Zoe, Leilani, Buffy, Willow, Ace, and Ivy-Lou.

Made in the USA
Columbia, SC
10 September 2022

66863428R00040